3/95

Five-Minute
FRIGHTS

Five-Minute FRIGHTS

By William A. Walker, Jr.

Illustrated by
Will Suckow and Martin Charlot

STERLING PUBLISHING CO., INC.

New York

Library of Congress Cataloging-in-Publication Data Available

10 9 8 7 6 5 4 3 2 1

Published by Sterling Publishing Company, Inc.
387 Park Avenue South, New York, NY 10016
© 1994 by RGA Publishing, Inc.
Distributed in Canada by Sterling Publishing
c/o Canadian Manda Group, P.O. Box 920, Station U
Toronto, Ontario, Canada M8Z 5P9
Distributed in Great Britain and Europe by Cassell PLC
Villiers House, 41/47 Strand, London WC2N 5JE, England
Distributed in Australia by Capricorn Link (Australia) Pty Ltd.
P.O. Box 6651, Baulkham Hills, Business Centre, NSW 2153, Australia

Sterling ISBN 0-8069-0764-9 Trade
0-8069-0765-7 Paper

To Andrew Friedman,
my first fan and favorite critic.

—W.A.W., Jr.

Table of Contents

Rites of Passage

illy Bishop's eyes lit up as he tore the wrapping paper off his birthday presents. They were everything he'd wanted: a coal-black Dracula cape, a set of lifelike fangs, and a large tombstone his father had cast from cement. He'd wanted a coffin, too, but his parents had buried that idea. That was okay. This stuff was neat. Especially the tombstone. Though made of concrete, it gleamed just like polished granite and had a real cool bloodstain on the front. But the coolest part yet was what it said:

Here lies
COUNT DRACULA
1745–?

For as long as he could remember, Billy had loved watching those old monster movies on TV. Frankenstein, the Wolfman, and Dracula were his friends, and certainly better friends than the creeps at school. They called him a weirdo and a freak just because he was curious about monsters and scary things.

With a gleeful shout and caped arms outstretched, Billy ran around the room, flashing his fangs like the Count himself.

"I vant to drink your blood," he said, swooping

down in front of his mother, drawing the cape around his face.

"That's nice," she said, offering her neck.

"Aw, Mom. You're supposed to scream and faint!"

"Sorry, honey, I forgot."

Billy rolled his eyes. Parents were never any fun. Then, remembering the tombstone, he got an idea.

"Mom? Can I put up the tombstone in the backyard? Please?" He took off his fangs and looked soulful.

"Yes, dear," she said, smiling warmly. "But don't stay out too long. It'll be getting dark soon."

Walking with his hands stretched stiffly before him like a zombie, Billy said, "It shall be done." Then he grabbed the tombstone, got a trowel from the garage, and streaked out into the Connecticut twilight.

The Bishop farm took up several acres and had a pond and a couple of fields. Near the pond was the place Billy loved most. It was a small glade surrounded by twisted ash trees and huge, dark bushes. At night, when the mist came off the pond and the moon shone down, the clearing looked just like a scene in *Swamp Thing* or *Night of the Living Dead.*

Choosing a level spot he'd be able to see from his bedroom, Billy dug a small trench with the trowel and pressed the tombstone into the soft soil. Then he tilted it just the right amount and stood back. It was perfect.

That night, Billy lay awake waiting for the moon to rise. When he saw its pale beams crawling along his bedroom floor, he rushed to the window, looked out, and smiled. Dracula's tombstone shone like a bone-chilling beacon in the clearing, the bloodstain looking dark and rich. The mist moved lazily across the ground,

and the bare ash trees sighed in the breeze.

Billy's eyes widened as he saw something move in the swirling mist. *Was somebody out there?* He rubbed his eyes and looked again. He could just make out two figures near the tombstone. *What were they doing?*

Curious, Billy crawled out the window and bounded across the field to the clearing, hiding himself behind a small tree. And then he recognized the people in front of his tombstone. It was his mother and father!

"Mom . . . Dad. What's going on?"

His parents stopped their digging, stood up straight, and turned toward him. Billy gasped as he saw their faces. Their eyes pulsed with a fiery red glow and their fangs gleamed dully in the moonlight. They were like something out of a nightmare.

"Look, son!" his father said excitedly, twirling his cape over the tombstone.

The inscription on the tombstone had changed. No longer a toy, it now read:

Here lies
BILLY BISHOP
1983–1994

"NO!" Billy screamed as he staggered backwards.

Walking up to Billy, his mother put her arms around him and said, "It's time, dear."

Billy shrieked and ran back toward the house. Suddenly his parents were there in front of him.

"NO!" he yelled. But his father's hands were clutching at his throat. Billy felt dizzy as he looked into his glowing face. Then, in the blink of an eye, he found himself looking up at his parents from the bottom of a hole. They stood over him, smiling warmly as they picked up the shovels.

"All vampires must die before their rebirth," his father said, his voice sounding raspy and hollow. "It's time to come meet your whole family."

Unable to move, Billy watched helplessly as his parents began to fill in the hole. He screamed and screamed until the heavy soil covered his tear-streaked face.

Muffy's Back

Muffy came back the first time last week. Everyone was sad after that big old truck squashed her flat. Even Mom cried at the funeral. It wasn't like a real funeral, not like Auntie June's last summer. At hers there were lots of pretty flowers, and lots to eat afterwards, and everyone cried.

We buried Muffy in the backyard and my little brother, Cary, made a neat little marker with her name on it. Every day for a week I visited her grave and put a flower on it. Then one day I went to visit and found nothing but a hole that looked all ripped and ragged, like the earth had upchucked. I was really upset and sure that Ralph, the big retriever next door, had dug Muffy up. And then I heard Mom scream.

I ran inside and found her on the floor. She'd struck her head on the counter and blood was all over the place. And right there, lapping up the mess, was Muffy. She had a crazy glint in her one cloudy eye and her head still had that funny misshapen look it had after the accident. Her tail hung limply, broken in several places, and I could see a couple of her ribs poking through her torn skin. I gasped and Muffy stopped lapping up the blood, looked up, and hissed at me, her teeth yellow and sharp. She looked so angry, so fierce, like she hated my guts.

14

I screamed and the cat took off. I looked for her awhile, but she was still gone by the time the ambulance took my mom away to the hospital.

"What scared your mother?" Daddy kept asking me. I wanted to tell him that Muffy came back from the dead, but I knew he wouldn't believe me. I just prayed that Muffy would go somewhere—wherever dead cats go—and never come back.

But Muffy didn't go away.

I heard her yowling at the moon that night and saw her at my window, her one good eye glowing a fiery green. She had that funny look she used to get when I forgot to feed her or left her out overnight.

"Go away!" I screamed. But Muffy just stared at me and hissed, like she was laughing at me. She was gone in the morning.

I spent all day at school worrying about my mom. The doctors said that she'd had some kind of seizure and might need a full-time nurse. Daddy was crying and I felt bad again about not telling him about Muffy. But what good would it do, anyway?

Finally, I decided to tell him. It was like I had to get it out whether he believed me or not.

"How can you say that, Penny?" my dad said, and then he put his arm around me. "Your mother is real sick, sweetheart. I know you're upset, but it's not a good time to make up stories."

I got all weepy then, and tried to convince him, but he wouldn't listen. Finally, he just got a sad look on his face and started to read the paper.

But I knew Muffy would be back and I had to do something.

That night I put my dresser in front of my window. But Muffy didn't come back for me. She got Cary while he was asleep, tore out his throat. No one could figure out how it happened, how someone could've gotten in through locked windows. My poor little brother looked so lost and frightened with his face all screwed up into that hideous, silent scream.

Daddy's in the hospital now, too. He'd taken to wandering the neighborhood late at night, shrieking and crying at the top of his lungs. And this afternoon a nice lady picked me up from the Jessups' next door and brought me to this great big place with lots of other kids.

I hear the grown-ups whisper about me. They think I killed Cary and hurt my mom.

They think I'm crazy.

But Muffy's the real killer . . . and she hates me.

She hates me for all those missed meals and all the times I dressed her up in doll clothes. She hates me like only the dead can hate. Every night after everyone's asleep, and the moon shines through the bars on my window, I hear Muffy crying for me. Every night she gets closer . . . and closer . . . and closer. I'm writing this down so everyone will know the truth. Everyone will know that Muffy's come back.

And now she's coming for me. . . .

Carnival of Terror

Donny's face dropped as he pocketed the ten dollars his mother had given him and trudged out of the house, her words still on his mind: "You boys are to use this money to go to the movies, not the carnival. Is that understood?"

She made him feel like a little kid and he was already thirteen. And worst of all, she'd read him like a book. She knew the carnival had come to town and would only be there one day. She knew he'd rather go to the carnival than to a movie he could go to anytime.

The farther he got from home, the more that money burned in his pocket. By the time he met his friend Jerry in front of the theater, he'd made up his mind.

"No way," Jerry said when Donny told him he planned on going to the carnival anyway. "My mom'll kill me if I'm not here when she comes to pick me up."

"She'll never know," Donny said. "Come on. It'll be a blast."

Again, Jerry shook his head, so Donny left him there in front of the theater. "Go on, wait for your mommy," he taunted. "I'm going to have some fun."

The Barrabus Carnival and Travelling Fun Show stood on the fairgrounds outside of town, looking somewhat worn around the edges. Its tents were patched and faded, and the rides looked more rickety than they should.

"Boy, what a cheesy carnival," Donny said to himself, suddenly sorry he'd come.

"Come one, come all and see creatures so horrifying that no one can bear the sight of them! Do you dare to look on Alligator Man, Rat Woman, or Magnetron the Magnificent?"

The barker called out his pitch, trying to entice the small crowd inside. Donny found himself drawn to the shabby tent along with a dozen other curious kids. Near the entrance stood faded paintings of the exhibits inside. To Donny they looked kind of silly.

"How much?" he asked the barker.

"To see these living wonders?" the man said, looking him up and down. "For you, only a dollar." The man smiled. "Are you game?"

Donny shrugged, paid the creepy-looking man the dollar, and joined the others inside.

But as soon as he saw the "exhibits," he got very angry. Alligator Man was some guy

19

in a green vinyl suit with a papier mâché alligator head over his own. Rat Woman had fake fur plastered all over her body, huge false buckteeth, and silly whiskers. And Magnetron the Magnificent was just some goofy-looking nerd whose hair stood out from static electricity.

"You're all a bunch of fakes!" he yelled.

Storming out of the tent, Donny decided to try the haunted house ride. If that proved to be stupid as well, he would go home. Outside the haunted house stood a deserted cotton candy stand. Donny helped himself, leaving a quarter on the counter to ease his conscience.

As he settled into one of the cars that would take him through the haunted house, he decided he would definitely go home after the ride was over. The jerking motion of the car made him a little queasy, and the moth-eaten witches, ghosts, and goblins that leaped out at him wouldn't have scared his baby brother. He was getting pretty tired, too, and as if things weren't bad enough, the cotton candy tasted weird. He ate it anyway since it turned out to be the only enjoyable part of the ride.

Struggling to stay awake, Donny tried to climb out of the car. Why was he so sleepy? Then, just as he figured out the cotton candy must have been drugged, he collapsed into a heap.

"Come one, come all and see creatures so horrifying that no one can bear the sight of them! They will thrill you, chill you, dazzle the mind, and freeze the soul! Never have we had so fantastic a selection as we do today! Come see and hear their amazing tales!"

The voice of the barker brought him around. How long had he been out? No way to tell. Boy, did his head ache! Opening his eyes, he found himself in a dim and gloomy room. He reached out into the darkness and his hand curled around something cold and metallic.

Bars.

He was in one of the cages!

Jumping up, he stifled a scream, imagining himself trapped with the Rat Woman or Alligator Man. But as his eyes adjusted to the gloom, he found himself alone. It was then he heard the murmuring voices. Pressing himself against the bars, he could just make out the shapes of people in the murky room beyond.

"Hey! Let me out of here!" he hollered.

"Hear that?" the barker bellowed. "It is the cry of Human Boy! Feast your eyes!"

The lights snapped on, blinding Donny. The crowd gasped and he heard several women screaming. Then his eyes adjusted and Donny's screaming joined the crowd's.

Outside the bars stood a group of creatures that defied description. All of them had green scaly skin and four giant bulging eyes popping out of two, sometimes three misshapen heads!

"Yes, folks! Never in the history of the Barrabus Carnival and Travelling Fun Show have we had a specimen such as this! Now, come along and see 'The Singing Worm of Alpha Centauri,' one of the most incredible creatures known in the Galaxy. . . ."

Dead Giveaway

ou've put on too much rouge," Jarrod Pomeroy said patiently. "Use a lighter touch."

Philip smiled and nodded at the mortician and began applying the makeup correctly.

"That's perfect, Philip, that's just right."

Philip puffed up with pride as he finished the makeup on old Mrs. Hornsby. She looked a lot better now than she did when she came in. In the year since his parents had died in that car accident, he'd taken to hanging around the funeral home. Mr. Pomeroy and his wife were real nice. They'd taken him under their wing and treated him like the son they never had. And to top it all off, he was learning a trade, and a fascinating one at that.

Pomeroy's Funeral Parlor sat in the center of town and always seemed to have a steady flow of business. As part of his new education, Philip was allowed to dress and make up the bodies. But the embalming and reconstruction, if any, was left to "Uncle" Jarrod. Philip would watch with fascination as Mr. Pomeroy removed all the blood and pumped in the foul-smelling fluid that kept the bodies fresh just long enough to plant them in the ground. People never realized how fast the bodies would rot if not for Mr. Pomeroy's expert touch.

Philip was sorry that Mr. Pomeroy didn't keep the

bodies around longer. He really felt like he got to know these people after awhile, and it was such a heart-break to see them carted off and buried. Sometimes, late at night, Philip would sneak over to the home, using his own key to get inside. He would sit for hours and talk to the corpses laid out in their coffins, their faces in peaceful repose. He knew they couldn't answer him back, but he somehow felt they heard him just the same, and appreciated not being left alone in the dark.

"Philip," Jarrod said one morning, "I received a call last night that Mrs. Benson passed away, and her daughter is all broken up about it. Since Henrietta is out at the market, would you keep the daughter company until I join you?"

"Yes, sir, Uncle Jarrod," Philip said, smiling brightly.

Right at two o'clock, Regina Benson arrived to make the arrangements for her mother. A thin, color-less woman, she cried into a limp handkerchief as Philip smiled and led her into his uncle's gloomy office.

"Don't worry, Miss Benson," Philip said, "we'll take good care of your mother. I'll make sure she looks completely natural."

The grief-stricken woman looked at the small thir-teen-year-old boy with a startled expression. "What?" she said. "Is this some kind of a joke?"

Before Philip could answer, Mr. Pomeroy appeared in the doorway.

"Miss Benson," he said, sweeping into the room. "How sorry I am for your loss."

Upon seeing her angry expression, his own became troubled. "Is something wrong?"

"It is, indeed! I didn't know it was the habit of this

establishment to allow children to work on the bodies!"

Jarrod's face fell and Philip suddenly felt awful. With his eyes filling with tears, Philip ran from the room and rushed up the stairs to the living quarters. He sat on a small overstuffed sofa in the hallway and covered his face with his hands. Mr. Pomeroy had warned him not to tell people he did the makeup. Now the kind old man could lose his license.

Feeling more and more guilty, he decided to run away. He jumped to his feet, dashed to the stairs, and collided with Mr. Pomeroy, who was just coming up. With a startled cry, the man toppled over backwards, tumbling head over heels down the long flight of stairs. His body made a sickening thud as it came to rest at the bottom of the stairs. He lay there unmoving, his head twisted halfway around, a look of pained surprise on his face.

"Oh, no!" Philip gasped.
"No, no, no!"

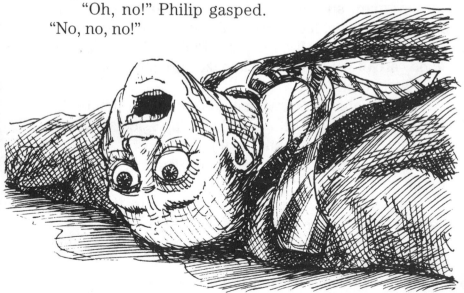

It was then that he heard Mrs. Pomeroy's car turn into the driveway.

Panicking, Philip grabbed a comic book, ran into the kitchen, and pretended to read, his heart racing. Moments later Mrs. Pomeroy breezed in, laden with grocery bags.

"Where is Mr. Pomeroy?" she asked cheerfully.

Philip smiled weakly, trying to appear calm. "I—I think he might be in the office."

"Oh, okay," she replied. "Would you mind putting away the groceries while I speak to him?"

"Yes—no—I mean . . . sure."

Philip began unloading the bags and waited to hear Mrs. Pomeroy's screams.

A minute ticked by . . . then another . . . and another . . . nothing.

Unable to stand it any longer, Philip crept out of the kitchen and peered into the hallway. He stifled a gasp as he saw Mrs. Pomeroy dragging her husband's body into the embalming room.

"Jarrod, Jarrod, Jarrod," she scolded. "You're such a clumsy oaf. What am I to do with you?"

Philip shook his head, trying to make sense of it all. Was she crazy? Couldn't she see he was dead?

With curiosity overcoming his fear, Philip walked into the embalming room and stopped dead in his tracks. Mrs. Pomeroy had Jarrod on the worktable and was hooking him up to the embalming machine. Noticing Philip out of the corner of her eye, she turned and smiled. The woman had lost none of her cheerfulness.

"Philip," she said, pointing toward the embalming machine, "be a dear and turn that on, would you?"

25

All he wanted to do was to run screaming from the room, but Philip shuffled over to the embalming machine in a daze and flipped on the switch. It coughed once and began chugging away as it pumped the amber-colored fluid into Jarrod Pomeroy's lifeless body. Within seconds the color returned to the dead man's face and he began breathing. A moment later, he opened his eyes, sat up, and grinned.

Philip nearly fainted.

Jarrod got off the table and turned to his wife. "Thank you, dear," he said, cracking his neck back into place. "You were just in time."

Mrs. Pomeroy scowled. "Jarrod! How many times do I have to tell you not to die where the clients can see you!"

"I'm sorry, dear. The boy and I had a little mishap," Mr. Pomeroy said, turning to fix Philip with a studied gaze. "Now that our little secret is out, I think it's only fair to let Philip share it with us." The horrible man's smile turned predatory as he climbed off the table and approached the wide-eyed boy. "After all," he said, "the dead never give anything away."

The Gold Watch

he old man looked frail and wasted in the hospital bed, though his eyes shined with love as he gazed at the young boy standing shyly by the door.

"Come closer, Benny," he said, his voice a papery whisper.

Benny looked to his parents, who sat by the bed, their faces etched with concern. They nodded. Benny hated seeing his Grandpa looking so old and sick. He wanted him back just like the days not so long ago when they fished and played catch together down by the small creek that ran through their property.

Benny edged closer, his heart in his throat. Would he catch something if he got too close? The old man smiled as Benny reached the bedside, but his smile made his face look like a grinning skull.

"I have something for you, Benny," he said.

The old man reached under the covers and pulled out a small wooden box. It was beautifully carved and on the top it had two engraved letters. One letter was familiar, the other quite strange: AΩ. The old man's hands trembled as he opened the box. Benny bent forward, his eyes opening in delight and awe. Sitting on the white satin interior was a gold watch. Instead of numbers, dazzling jewels ringed the face. At the twelve

o'clock position there were the same two letters: AΩ.

The old man pressed the watch into Benny's hands, his eyes burning with intensity. "Guard this well, my boy. With it you will do amazing things."

Benny had tears in his eyes as he grasped the cool metal. "I will, Grandpa. I will."

"But promise me you will use it wisely," the old man said, clutching Benny's arm. "And listen to me carefully now, boy. I have to explain something very important about that watch. You must be remember never to—" But suddenly the old man lurched into a coughing fit and collapsed against his pillows.

A nurse rushed in. "I'm sorry," she said, "but everyone will have to leave."

* * *

Benny sat in his room that night, staring at the watch in his hands. It was neat, but he'd rather have his grandfather back than some old watch. Turning it over, he noticed an inscription:

Tick-tock, counterclock,
Forward march and backward walk,
Pull the stem and turn the hands,
Travel to past and future lands.

What on earth did that mean? And what did the weird letters stand for? Benny raised the watch to his ear. Nothing. Must have to wind it, he thought. Benny felt a tingle in his hands as he pulled out the stem. He twisted it, watching the hands go round and round. What time was it? He glanced at the glowing letters of his digital clock: 8:33. He set the hands and pushed in the stem.

Suddenly the room flooded with light and grew dark again. Benny heard his mother crying. Alarmed, he ran downstairs and found his father holding his mother as she sobbed uncontrollably.

"What's wrong?" Benny asked, wide-eyed with fear.

"Grandpa died this afternoon," his father said.

His mother cried harder.

"But, Dad! We saw Gramps this afternoon."

His father gave him a strange look. "Benny, that was *yesterday.*"

Stunned, Benny ran back upstairs and grabbed the watch. He'd moved the hands forward and gone a day *forward* in time. Maybe the watch could bring his grandfather back, too! Pulling out the stem, he turned the hands backwards, going round and round and round. Finally, after turning it back 365 times, he stopped, held his breath, and pushed in the stem.

As the days wound backward, the room flashed from bright to dark. After what felt like forever, the flashing stopped. Benny ran to the window and gasped as he saw his grandfather hunched over the fishing pole by the creek. Grabbing the watch, he thrust it into his pocket. The back door slammed as he ran out of the house.

"Grandpa! Grandpa!" he yelled.

The old man turned and looked, the smile dying on his lips.

"Benny. You must go, quickly!" he said as the bewildered young boy reached him.

"But why, Grandpa, why?"

"Because you do not belong here. Your *younger* self does."

"What?" Benny said.

"Grandpa, I found some worms!" a young boy's voice called in the distance.

The old man looked horrified as a younger Benny came running around the back of the house.

"Quickly, Benny, you must not *see* each other!"

Angered, Benny pulled out the watch and began winding it forward. "I only wanted you back, Grandpa!" As Benny furiously wound the watch, the large hand suddenly broke off. "Here! Take your old watch. I don't want it!"

"NO, BENNY!" his grandfather screamed as Benny hurled the watch at a large rock. It landed against the stone and smashed into a million glittering pieces.

Suddenly everything began to flash and sputter, like a motor trying to catch. Horrified, Benny watched as the world around him began to speed up until it became a dizzying blur. He stared with terrified eyes as the years flew past with no signs of stopping. He saw his parents grow old, his brother get married in the backyard.

On and on and on. Faster and faster. His father was in a hospital bed now. His aged mother was crying.

"NOOOOOOO!" he screamed.

In the blink of an eye, his house disintegrated, replaced by another, more modern and bizarre. A split second later, it too fell to dust. Days zoomed by like the flash of a strobe light.

On and on and on.

For Benny, trapped in a lonely eternity all his own, time would forever remain a blur, a ghostly, fleeting thing, as he moved ever forward . . . to infinity.

The Screaming Skeleton

o any of you know what the *tibia* is?"

Mr. Bertram's third period biology class stared back at him blankly, their eyes round as saucers.

"No one? All right, let's bring in Mr. Bones and let him answer our question." The class snickered when their teacher wheeled out the old skeleton. Yellowed and brittle with age, it hung from a rolling stand, the bones all connected by pins and bits of twisted wire.

Kenny sighed with boredom. *Not this stuff again,* he thought. He was sick and tired of seeing this old bag of bones every time Bertram wanted to illustrate a point. Once, as a gag, Kenny had tried to take it apart. He still bore the small scar from the wire that gashed his skin. He should've smashed the old skeleton while he had the chance.

Suddenly Kenny heard Mr. Bertram ask him a question. Stupefied—since he hadn't heard a word Bertram had been saying—Kenny looked anxiously around the room for a moment, then finally shrugged weakly.

Bertram stared at him. "Kenny, maybe if you paid attention in class, you'd learn something."

Kenny turned scarlet and stared at his desktop.

"Yeah, kid, pay attention!"

Kenny's head snapped up as he tried to figure out

32

who the wise guy was. But everyone was watching Mr. Bertram.

"Now then," the teacher said, lifting one of the skeleton's legs. "The tibia is the long bone between the knee and the foot. Very often when you break this bone it is known as a 'compound fracture.' That's when the bone pokes out through the skin."

"Gross!" someone yelled, causing a wave of nervous laughter.

"I know it sounds awful, but our skeletons are really remarkable in their way. And we couldn't get along without them. Not only do they hold us together, but their marrow creates our blood cells . . ."

Kenny closed his eyes and began to daydream about his new baseball glove.

"Hey, kid! Wake up!"

Kenny's eyes snapped open and darted around the room. *Who said that?* He turned, expecting to see that meathead Joey Lewis trying to play one of his lame jokes. But Joey sat in the back of the room, his eyes focused on one of his comic books. Kenny shook his head and reached into his book bag.

"Over here, kid!"

This time he heard it for sure. And he realized who it was.

Mr. Bones.

Kenny gasped, feeling panicked. The old skeleton was actually talking to him. Didn't anyone else hear it? Maybe he was going nuts. He stared hard at the gleaming skull, willing it to say something again, ready to leap up and smash it to dust. But Mr. Bones just hung there, smiling stupidly like the dead thing that it was.

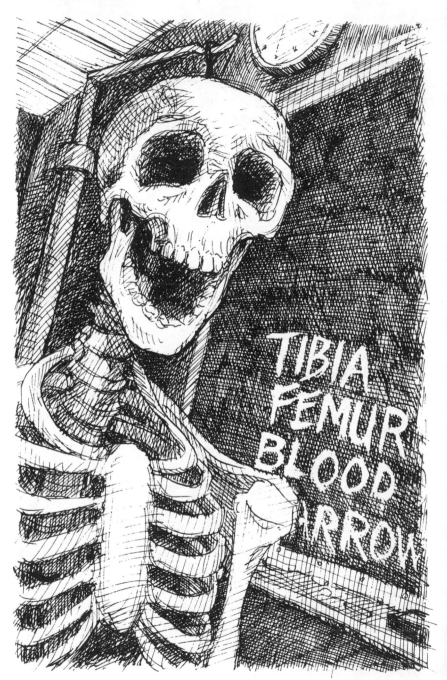

Or was it dead?

After school, Kenny stayed behind, lingering in the boy's room until most everyone had gone home. Creeping out of the lavatory, he snuck into Bertram's classroom. There hung Mr. Bones, smiling his lipless grin.

"So, kid, you come for some extra credit?"

Kenny sneered at the skeleton. "Yeah, right. Why don't you just shut up?"

"Make me, you little pip-squeak!" Mr. Bones screeched.

Kenny smiled and reached for the old skeleton. He wrenched the skull off the rest of the bones and hurled it against the wall. As it smashed into jagged fragments, Kenny heard Mr. Bones scream in pain. Good. The old fossil deserved it. But Kenny's smile of triumph faltered as the screaming continued, earsplitting and unceasing. Realizing that the janitor might come in at any moment, Kenny ran from the room and headed for home.

But the screaming didn't stop. On and on it went inside Kenny's head as if, somehow, Mr. Bones had taken up residence there. It was like having his own personal cat fight inside his skull. All through dinner Kenny tried to ignore the persistent shrieks that only he could hear, but it got harder and harder.

"Are you all right, dear?" his mother asked, noting her son's pained expression.

Kenny winced. "I don't feel very well," he said. "I think I'll go to bed."

He trudged up the stairs, all the while hearing Mr. Bones bellowing in his head. If it didn't stop soon, he

35

would go mad.

Exhausted, Kenny dropped onto the bed and somehow fell asleep. But just a few hours later he awoke. The screaming was louder than ever. He held his head between his hands and cried, "Stop it! Stop it, now!"

Miraculously, the screaming stopped and Kenny breathed easier . . . until a headless Mr. Bones walked into the room. The horrible skeleton appeared to glow, and Kenny could hear the old bones clacking together like dry twigs.

"So, you had enough of me, kid?" Mr. Bones asked.

"Yes!" Kenny exclaimed. "Go away. I'll do anything."

"Well, seein' as how you broke my head, I'll be needin' another one."

"Sorry, I'm fresh out of dried-up skulls," Kenny said.

"That's okay," Mr. Bones said, coming closer. *"I'll take a fresh one."*

With the swiftness of a cat, Mr. Bones grabbed Kenny's head and tore it from his body, then jammed it onto his own empty neck.

CREEPY-CRAWLY

Bugs!" Sharon screamed as she saw the thin line of ants marching across the picnic blanket.

"Now, honey, they won't hurt you. They're just helping themselves to our leftovers," her mother said.

Sure enough, Sharon spied bread crumbs and other bits of their meal clutched in the ants' tiny jaws as they moved off into the grass. Sharon's face twisted in disgust. Jumping to her feet, she began stomping on the ants, her eyes burning with frightened intensity. The tiny creatures scurried in confusion, trying to avoid the crush of her giant foot.

"Sharon!" her mother shouted, alarmed at her daughter's behavior.

But the girl ignored her, totally caught up in her frenzy. When the last of the ants were dead or gone, she finally calmed down. "I *hate* bugs," she said emphatically.

And so she did. As long as she could remember, Sharon had hated the ugly little "creepy-crawlies," as she called them. Even butterflies gave her the willies as they fluttered around the garden behind the house. But she especially hated spiders and roaches, the bugs that scuttled out of sight when the lights were switched on.

Every night Sharon would take her flashlight and search under the bed. If something crawled there, she had her can of bug spray ready. Only when they were all dead could she go to sleep. Then, in the morning, she shook out her shoes to see if anything had nested there from the last time she wore them, shivering if something fell out. She even pretended to be sick so she could stay home from school the week her science teacher discussed insects and their benefits to the planet.

But it was her "bug hunts" that Sharon lived for. That afternoon, when they returned home from the picnic, Sharon grabbed her can of bug spray and headed into the basement. It didn't matter that her mother hired a service to come in and spray for insects, Sharon always found more. Always.

"Where are you going, Sharon?" her mother asked, seeing her daughter's determined look.

"Bug hunting."

"Honey, why don't you leave them alone?"

Sharon stared at her mother in disbelief. Why would anyone want to save bugs? Grabbing a flashlight, she descended into the dark basement. The beam caught a family of roaches in the middle of the floor.

"Got ya!" she yelled, blasting them with the spray. They twitched and squirmed as the lethal liquid covered their bodies. Leaving them behind, Sharon tiptoed around the room, beaming the flashlight around as she looked for more prey.

In a corner she found a spider in its web, about to devour a fly. She destroyed them both without thinking twice.

"Those men did not spray good enough, Mom!" Sharon shouted.

Her mother didn't answer. Suddenly Sharon heard

38

something and whirled, stabbing the darkness with her flashlight.

More roaches!

Her eyes widened in fury as she spied a dozen or more of the wretched bugs scurrying for cover. Quickly she squashed or sprayed as many as she could, missing a couple that disappeared into holes in the walls.

"I'll get you!" she yelled. "Just you wait."

That night, the bug patrol turned up two spiders and a roach. More than usual. Sharon bit her lip as she climbed under the sheets. She wondered if she should keep the can of bug spray under her pillow. But the spray was expensive and her mother refused to buy any more. In fact, Sharon had spent all her saved-up allowance on bug spray, and her last can was running out.

Snapping off her bedside light, she lay under the covers, stiff as a board. It was always like this. Waiting . . . waiting to feel something crawl across her skin. Soon her eyes grew heavy and she drifted off to sleep.

She gasped as she bolted awake. What was wrong? *Something* was wrong. She reached for her light and felt tiny legs scuttle across her hand. Stifling a scream, Sharon grabbed for the spray.

It was gone!

In terror, she snapped on her light and found herself living her worst nightmare. The floor was swimming with insects of every description: spiders, ants, roaches, silverfish, millipedes, beetles, and bugs she couldn't even identify, horrible slithery things that made her stomach turn.

She tried to shout for help, but her words came

out a strangled whisper.

It was then that she saw the first wave of bugs creeping over the edge of her bed. She could see their antennae waving furiously, their tiny jaws snapping in anticipation. Closer and closer they came, thousands of legs moving with grim determination.

"No," she whimpered, huddling against the headboard, tears flooding her eyes. "I didn't *mean* it."

On they came.

As the first bug touched the bare skin of her feet, she found her voice and let out a bloodcurdling scream.

"What was that?" her father said, waking with a start.

Sharon's mother sighed. "Oh, Sharon probably saw a roach on the floor."

Her father shook his head. "I'm going to have a talk with her. This bug nonsense has gotten out of hand."

Pulling on his bathrobe, he stalked across the hall and opened the door to Sharon's room. Then he stopped cold, staring in mute horror at the scene before him. The skeleton of his daughter lay on her bed, picked clean of skin and muscle. He never noticed the thousands of eyes that watched him hungrily from the crevices of the room. They stirred and began to move toward him. Now that they had tasted flesh, they would never be satisfied with bread crumbs again.

The Crystal Coffin

I dare you!" Jimmy said, crossing his arms and looking smug.

"No way," Terry said. "I *double* dare you!"

The two went nose to nose, their eyes burning with challenge. The rest of the group held their breath. Finally, Terry backed down, his face flushed and his eyes everywhere but on Jimmy.

"All right," Jimmy said, flushed with triumph. "Then we go tonight. Terry goes in first."

Everyone murmured. Terry stayed silent, scared. Suddenly he perked up. "Hey! What about the new kid?"

All eyes turned to Janos, a small dark-haired boy with soulful brown eyes. He'd moved into the neighborhood a couple of days before, and the gang had let him hang around even though his nerdy clothes and formal way of speaking made him stand out. Now he edged away from everyone, a look of uncertainty on his delicate face.

Jimmy smiled and cuffed Terry on the side of the head. "Good idea. For once you're using your brain." Jimmy sauntered over to the small boy.

"What's your name, kid?" Jimmy demanded with authority.

"Janos," the boy whispered.

Everyone broke out laughing. The boy turned beet red and hung his head.

"Jamnose, huh? What kind of ninny name is that?"

Janos clamped his lips tightly and stared at the ground.

"Look at me!" Jimmy said, grabbing him by his shirt. "You're going with us."

Janos snapped his head up, his eyes filling with fear.

"W where?" he stammered.

"To the old Barnaby place," Jimmy said, his voice sounding as ominous as he could make it.

Everyone knew that the old Barnaby house was haunted. It sat up on a hill overlooking the town, like some prehistoric bird of prey waiting to pounce on its victim. Rumor had it that the last owner, an old woman, had been laid to rest in the basement in a coffin made of crystal. Tonight, the Elm Street Gang would find out for sure.

"Not tonight!" Janos said in a small voice.

Jimmy whirled on Janos and stared menacingly into the boy's dark eyes. "Tonight or never, Jamnose. You wanna be in the gang, don't ya?"

Janos nodded quickly. Jimmy smiled a serpent's grin.

"Good. We'll be at your house at 11:30. Be ready."

Janos frowned as he watched the other boys strutting away. Then, as soon as they were out of sight, a slight smile crept over his face.

At 11:30 sharp the boys showed up at Janos's house and the group headed out.

They took a route straight through the woods.

The moon shone down with a ghostly light as they pushed their way past the gnarled branches that scraped their arms and tore at their clothes. Then, there it was! Three stories tall with a stone tower at each corner, the old house looked like a medieval castle. The moon reflected off the windows, which looked like dozens of evil eyes. Suddenly an owl screeched and the boys nearly jumped out of their skins.

"I don't know about this, Jimmy," Terry said, his voice quavering.

The others began objecting as well. "What's the matter? Are you all chicken?" Jimmy asked, angry to have his leadership challenged. "We're going inside! And Jamnose here is gonna lead the way."

Trembling, Janos shambled up the path toward the wide stone steps. The other boys followed. The immense carved door was slightly open, as if waiting for them. Janos pushed the heavy door, and it opened wider, its hinges groaning in protest. He snapped on a flashlight, illuminating some dusty old furniture and a long dark hallway. It looked like the open mouth of some large beast. Janos hesitated, and then, with a sudden air of confidence, he led the five boys to the basement entrance. Slowly, they followed him down the sagging stairway, jumping at every creak. At the bottom, they all stared at the fantastic sight before them. On a raised platform of sculpted stone was a beautiful crystal coffin. Even under a powdery layer of dust, the finely etched lead-crystal panels gleamed in the beam of Janos's flashlight, sending rainbow-colored spots dancing about the musty room.

"It's true," Terry gasped, running his hand over the stunning coffin. "Let's open it!"

Jimmy liked the idea. "Yeah. Let our pal, Jamnose, do it."

Surprisingly, the small boy needed no prodding. With reverent care, he lifted the lid. Inside the coffin lay the withered remains of a very old woman, her white beaded dress yellow with age. Gazing at the body with a curious tenderness, Janos bent and kissed the corpse on the lips.

"YUCK!" Terry said, shivering with disgust.

Jimmy and the rest of the gang stared in awestruck terror as the coffin filled with a bright, unearthly light. Before their eyes, the old woman turned from a dried-up mummy into a beautiful young girl with the same dark

45

eyes as Janos.

"Janos! You have come!" she said, her eyes shining with adoration.

"Yes. I wasn't sure it was time, but the others insist-ed," Janos said, fixing Jimmy and the others with a studied gaze.

"You have brought me some?" she asked.

"Five," Janos replied.

The girl turned, looked at the five frightened boys, and smiled. "Oh, Janos, they are perfect. *And I am so hungry.*"

Video of Death

Come on, Jilly, we haven't got all day," Tommy said.

But Jilly didn't hear her brother as her pretty green eyes scanned the shelves of videotapes. Video Palace was her home away from home, a place that held the keys to escape from the boring reality of school, homework, and ballet lessons.

"Mom is waiting for us," Tommy said. "Just pick a tape and let's go."

Jilly scowled at her brother. "Fine. Then you pick one."

Tommy grinned. "No problem," he said, racing off to the Horror section.

"All right!" Tommy said, grabbing a video.

Jilly fumed. Following him to the counter, she watched as the clerk examined the tape.

"You'll have to leave a deposit on this one," the clerk said. "Every time we rent this out, it never comes back and we have to buy a new one."

Tommy sighed. "How much?"

"Ten bucks . . . plus the rental . . . comes to $12.98."

"Wow," Tommy said. "Now I'm really curious." He pulled out the wrinkled twenty his mother had given him, paid the man, and walked out of the store with Jilly on his heels, protesting all the way.

Later that evening the family settled into the TV room and Tommy pushed the tape into the VCR.

"I just want it on record that Tommy picked this tape, not me," Jilly said.

"I figured as much," their father said as the title flashed on the screen: *Video Nightmares* in letters dripping blood.

"Oh, brother," Jilly said. "This is going to be nerdy."

"Now, Jilly," warned their mother, "let's give this a chance. It may be, well, entertaining."

Jilly rolled her eyes and settled onto the couch. Then, as the picture faded in, she found herself unable to talk, unable to breathe. There on the screen were she and Tommy—in the video store.

"Come on, Jilly, we haven't got all day."

Word for word, action for action, what had happened in the video store played itself out on the screen.

"How on earth did you two do this?" their mother cried with delight.

Tommy shrugged like it was no big deal. Jilly sat there, speechless. How *had* the video store done it? It looked professionally photographed and edited, just like a real movie.

The next scene grabbed everyone's attention, for it showed them all around the dinner table as they had been moments before. Before any of them could react, the scene shifted to the town graveyard as a rotted hand thrust up and out of the ground, followed by the most awful moaning sound.

Jilly and her family watched, horrified, as dozens of dead bodies ripped themselves out of the earth and began shuffling out of the graveyard. The scene cut

48

back to them seated around the TV.

"I just want it on record that Tommy picked this tape, not me."

The same words, the same actions repeated themselves on the screen. The scene then cut to the outside again as the army of dead people turned onto a residential street. Jilly realized that it was *their* street.

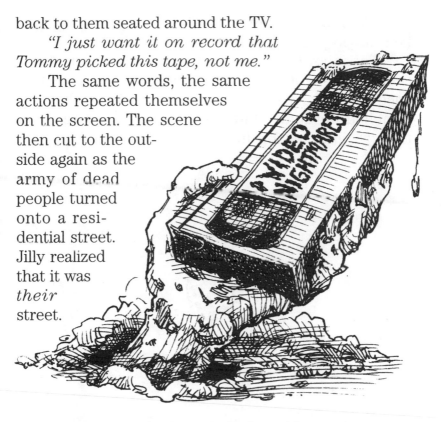

"Quick, pull out the tape!" she said.

"Quick, pull out the tape!"

Jilly gasped and Tommy reached for the VCR just as they heard someone—or something—scrabbling at the door.

"Break it, Tommy!" their mother said.

Tommy wrenched out the tape, threw it onto the floor, and stomped on it, feeling it crack into splinters under his weight. A foul-smelling vapor, accompanied by a terrible cackling, flowed out of the broken cassette.

"What was that?" their father asked.

"Who cares?" Tommy laughed, picking up the broken cassette. "It's toast now."

Then they heard the deep, unearthly moaning and the pounding of dozens of hands on the door. Jilly tried to hold back tears of panic as a panel on the door punched out and a hideously rotted hand reached through, grasping for the doorknob.

The Doll Maker

HELPERS WANTED
*Looking for two boys to help
with this year's parade float.
Will pay $10.00/hour.
555-5150. Ask for Mr. Zander.*

What do you think, Andy?" Eddie asked, with his lopsided grin.

Andy wrinkled his nose. "Old Man Zander has a doll shop. I don't want to work with a bunch of dolls. The guys will never let us live it down."

"Where else are you going to get that kind of money?" Eddie wanted to know.

Andy had to admit his friend was right. It wasn't easy for a thirteen-year-old boy to find a good summer job, let alone something that paid ten dollars an hour. He poked Eddie in the side. "Zander's shop is about ten blocks from here. Wanna race?"

Within minutes the two boys were standing in front of Zander's Zillions of Dolls, a rundown little shop nestled in the poorer section of town.

"Wow, this place looks like it's about to fall apart," Eddie said, picking off a piece of chipped paint.

"Yeah," Andy agreed. "I wonder how Mr. Zander can afford to pay ten dollars an hour."

Eddie shrugged. "Well, only one way to find out." He pushed open the door and a bell tinkled, signaling their arrival.

"Wow! This place is neat!" Eddie said, standing among dolls of every description—all dressed in costumes from countries all over the world.

A moment later, a gentle-looking old man with a white beard and crystal blue eyes came shuffling out of the back of the store.

"Ahh," he said, chuckling softly, "you've come to be my helpers, yes? Come, come."

The back of the store was even more impressive than the front. There were tools and machinery of all kinds. Doll parts hung from beams overhead—that gave the boys the creeps—but what drew their attention the most was the float.

"Whoa, a pirate ship!" Eddie exclaimed.

"With cannons and everything!" Andy said, giving his friend a high five.

"Is it not grand?" the old man asked proudly. "It has taken me years to build, but now with the parade only two days away, I need you boys to help put the crew together." Zander pointed to a pile of doll parts on the floor and continued. "Without the crew this float is nothing. Come, boys, let's get to work."

Over the next two days Andy and Eddie worked from 8:00 a.m. to dinnertime, putting together the big dolls and dressing them after Zander painted the faces and glued on the hair. Slowly but surely the float's crew came together, except for the pirate captain.

"Oh dear, I'm in trouble now," the old man said, his face saddened.

"What's wrong?" Eddie asked.

"I thought I had enough parts for the Captain, but as you can see, we're all out."

Andy followed his friend's gaze and saw the old man was right.

"What am I to do?" Zander asked, wringing his hands.

"Well, how about I take his place?" Eddie offered. "These dolls are as big as we are. I could wear the costume and stand on the float during the parade."

Zander's eyes lit up. "Why, I suppose you could!"

"Hey, Eddie, I don't know about this," Andy said, feeling kind of weird about the whole thing.

"Don't be such a drag," Eddie said. "It'll be fun. Mr. Zander can make you up, too."

Zander nodded enthusiastically, but Andy wanted no part of that.

"Aw, come on, Andy. We can both be on the float and wave at everyone!"

As usual, Andy caved in and went along. He watched, fascinated, as the makeup was applied to Eddie's face first. In a matter of minutes Eddie was totally transformed into the dashing pirate captain. Andy also noted that the makeup had run out.

"You snooze, you lose," Eddie said, twirling his pirate's moustache and grinning.

"I'm terribly sorry," Zander said. "I thought I had enough."

Andy shrugged. "That's okay. If it's all the same to you, I'll just watch the parade. Don't forget to wave, Captain Eddie."

But Eddie ignored him as Zander helped him into

54

his costume. Andy shrugged again and walked out of the shop.

* * *

The parade started right on time, just after 10:00 a.m. Andy watched and waited breathlessly for his friend to appear. Float after float came by—a tropical island float with pretty girls dancing the hula, a giant Trojan horse, a huge Bengal tiger, but no pirate ship and no Eddie. Finally, Andy spotted his friend as Mr. Zander's pirate ship rolled by, its crew standing at the ready. And there was Eddie, smiling a huge smile, looking like he was having such a blast that Andy found himself wishing there'd been more makeup.

"Hey, Eddie, way to go!" he shouted.

But Eddie stared straight ahead, as if he hadn't heard a thing. That was strange. "Hey, Eddie! Over here!" Andy yelled louder and waved.

The float glided by and not once did Eddie turn or wave. Andy became concerned and tried to fight his way through the crowd to keep up with his friend. But there were too many people and he gave up.

When the parade finally ended and the crowd thinned, Andy returned to the small shop. He found Zander puttering around behind the front counter.

"Ahh, Andy! We won the prize!" Zander's bright smile widened as he held up a garish trophy.

"That's great, Mr. Zander, but I'm looking for Eddie. Have you seen him?"

"Ahh, yes," Mr. Zander said, his eyes taking on a strange look. "He's in back."

Andy walked into the back room and quickly spotted his friend, sitting on a stool. He still wore the pirate captain's costume and that wild wide grin.

"Hey, buddy, we're going to be late—" But something about Eddie made Andy unable to finish his sentence. Maybe it was the paint peeling from one of his friend's cheeks. Or maybe it was the frozen look of terror in Eddie's unblinking eyes.

Andy gasped as Zander walked in behind him.

"Your friend was a real doll to help me the way he did," Zander smiled. "A real doll."

Double Trouble

here you are," their mother said as she tied the ribbon around Adelaide's hair. "My fine China dolls."

She smiled as she looked at her beautiful twin daughters, Angela and Adelaide. They were picture-perfect, the mirror image of each other. With dark black hair and lively green eyes, they would grow into heartbreakers. She was sure of that.

"You go and play now," she said, caressing Angela's face. "Dinner will be ready at six."

The two girls smiled prettily, left the room, and walked down the hall to the room they shared. Both of them were furious. It had always been like this. Their mother saw them as one girl in two bodies, but they were *different*. They *were!*

"What are we gonna do, Angie?" Adelaide said, sitting on her bed and staring at her sister, who sat across from her. "She still treats us like babies."

Angela flicked a strand of hair out of her eyes—something Adelaide hated.

"What do you expect, Addy, when you pull stunts like what you did to Mrs. Fenster's dog?"

Adelaide broke into the mischievous grin she always got. "Well, the little creep deserved it, always yapping like that. Besides, it hardly limps at all."

"And what about the time at school when you put that stuff into Bobby Jessup's chocolate milk. He almost *died!*"

Adelaide pouted. That always got their mother's sympathy and it drove Angela crazy. "I know . . . but wasn't it funny the way he turned blue and puked up all that icky stuff?" she said, giggling.

"Honestly, Addy, why can't you be nice?"

Adelaide's face clouded over. *"Honestly, Addy, why can't you be nice?"'* she said mockingly. "If I hear that one more time, *I'm* gonna puke."

Angela flicked her hair again. Adelaide fumed.

"How about you?" Adelaide said. "Little Miss Goody-Two-Shoes. Everyone *loves* little Angela. Little Angela *always* gets good grades. Little Angela's *so* perfect."

"I can't help it," Angela said, tears coming into her eyes. Her sister always knew how to get to her. She wished she could think of ways to hurt Adelaide, but it just wasn't in her.

Adelaide went over to her closet and started rummaging around. "Well, maybe it isn't your fault," she said over her shoulder. "But I'm sick of people thinking I'm you." She continued to dig for something, then suddenly let out a scream. She jumped back and, holding her hand, ran into the bathroom and slammed the door.

Angela stopped crying and ran after her sister. "Addy! What's wrong?" she yelled through the bathroom door.

"Nothing!" Adelaide shouted back, holding her bloody hand under the running faucet. "I just cut myself."

Angela shivered. She had a pretty good idea of what had happened. Her weird sister had probably cut herself on something in her "collection." She had snuck into her sister's closet one day and seen all the strange stuff Adelaide hoarded—jagged pieces of broken glass, a broken pair of scissors, even an old pocketknife that was so rusted it didn't close anymore. Why couldn't her sister collect something normal like dolls, or stamps, or stuffed animals? She collected all that stuff, but not Adelaide. *How could anyone think they were the same?*

The water stopped running and Adelaide stepped out of the bathroom with a bandage wrapped around her hand. She stepped closer to her sister and hugged her. "I'm sorry if I upset you, Angie," she said, a hard glint creeping into her eyes. "At least *we* know we're different—on the inside, anyway."

Angela pulled away from the embrace. "Well, I wish people could tell us apart from the outside, too."

A fiendish grin flashed on Adelaide's face. "Wow, Angie! Maybe we're more alike than I thought. I was just thinking the same thing. Follow me. I want to show you something." And with that, she walked quickly into their bedroom, Angela on her heels.

Adelaide opened her closet door. "I saw you peeking into my collection the other day." She held up her hand when she saw Angela about to speak. "But don't worry, sis. I don't mind. Especially now that I know you want to do the operation as much as I do."

"Operation?" Angela said, her voice shaking.

"Sure," said Adelaide. "And here are my tools. I've been collecting them for months." She displayed an array of sharp objects to Angela, who stared at them in

60

horror, unable to speak.

"I got these from Mom's sewing kit," Adelaide said, proudly holding up an innocent-looking needle and thread. "Perfect for suturing the cuts."

"Su-suturing?" stammered Angela.

"Yeah, silly. You wouldn't want to bleed to death, would you?"

Angela's heart began to pound wildly. "Mom!" she screamed and raced for the door.

But Adelaide was quicker. "Now why do you want to drag Mom into this?" she asked, blocking the door. "*She* wants to keep us the same. Besides, it was your idea to show how different we are . . . at least on the outside."

Stunned, Angela cringed in terror as her sister flashed a piece of broken glass in front of her face.

"This will make a lovely scar," said Adelaide, grabbing her sister. "Now hold still and try not to scream. We'll be different in no time."

Sarah's Last Wish

he black van skidded on the slick, wet pavement and the last thing Sarah remembered as it hurtled toward their car was the bright-colored sign painted on its side: THE GREAT MAGESTO—MAGICIAN AT LARGE. She barely had time to scream and then . . . blackness. She awoke a day or maybe a thousand days later, she didn't know which. As the fogginess of her vision cleared, she saw the relieved but worried faces of her parents hovering over her bed.

"Hello, sweetheart," her mother said. "How are you feeling?"

Sarah opened her mouth and tried to croak out an answer.

"It's all right, punkin," her father said, his own smile tight with concern. "Everything's going to be just fine."

"My head hurts," Sarah finally managed to say.

"It's nothing to get upset about, honey. The important thing is you're alive."

"What about Pammy and her mom?"

Her mother frowned and a look of sadness crept into her features. "Let's not talk about that now, dear. You need your rest."

Sarah began to cry, knowing that her mother was avoiding the horrible truth. Pammy must be dead.

They'd been coming back from ballet practice, some magician's van had run the stop sign, and then . . .

Why? Why did she get to live? Why did her best friend have to die?

Sarah was still in the hospital a month later. Finally, she was beginning to feel better and better. Enough, in fact, to crave a chocolate milk shake. "I can practically taste it," she said to herself. "I wish I had one right now."

"Surprise!" her mother said, poking her head inside the hospital room. "Look what I brought you! The doctor said it was all right, honey."

Her mother brought a paper bag out from behind her back and pulled out an ice-cold chocolate shake. Sarah drank it with relish, glad her mother had stopped treating her like a delicate piece of porcelain. Now if only she could get out of this depressing hospital.

"I wish I could go home, Mommy."

"I wish you could too, dear, but the doctor said at least two more weeks."

Sarah pouted as she returned to her shake.

A moment later, the doctor swept into the room, a smile on his tanned face. "You're looking wonderful, Sarah. I have some *very* good news for you. We're sending you home today. Right now, in fact."

Sarah smiled her most winning smile, not noticing her mother's startled look.

On her first day home, all her friends came by to visit, but as the day wore on, Sarah became more and more depressed. They were all talking about themselves and what they were doing. No one seemed to care about her. As the last of her friends left the room, her face clouded in anger. "I wish they would all go away for good," she said.

Moments later, she heard the sound of screeching brakes and metal hitting metal. She rushed to the window and saw two of her friends' bodies lying mangled in the street. Sarah's eyes widened in horror as she realized what had happened. She was responsible! She'd wished for her friends to go away for good, just like she'd wished for a milk shake and to leave the hospital. Tearing herself away from the window, Sarah threw herself onto the bed and wept.

After the ambulance drove off, her mother came in to check on her and found her daughter staring off into space, a look of deep grief on her face.

"That accident was my fault, Mom. I made a wish and it happened."

Her mother held her in her arms. "Nonsense, sweetheart. Things like that can't happen. It's all in your mind."

Sarah pulled away, angered. "That's what I mean! The doctor said I still had something they couldn't get out of my head. What is it, Mother?"

Her mother looked both pained and frightened.

"It's just a piece of lead crystal, sweetheart. The doctor said it should never cause any problems."

"What if it is causing problems? What if it's changed me? What if it's given me the power to make things happen . . . bad things?"

"Sarah, that's ridiculous. You're just imagining this."

"I AM NOT!" she screamed.

"Sarah, calm down, you're still not well."

"I will NOT calm down. All you and Dad ever do is

tell me I'm wrong. What I say is always wrong! Well,
I'm tired of that and I'm tired of you. I WISH I WERE
DEAD!"

* * *

Pammy tried to hold back a smile as they lowered Sarah's coffin into the ground. It was funny how things worked out. They both had pieces from that magician's crystal ball jammed into their brains from the accident, pieces the doctors dared not remove. Yet only Pammy had discovered the true extent of the crystal ball's secret power. In the instant before death had claimed her, Pammy had wished for life and had it miraculously restored. As she lay recuperating in her hospital bed, she realized she could do anything. She'd even been able to crawl inside Sarah's mind and make her wish for things, bad things that drove her to . . .

Pammy smiled, unable to stop herself. Now the lead in the ballet recital would be hers.

"Honey, why are you smiling?" her mother asked, concerned.

Pammy looked at her, thinking fast. "I was just thinking about all the good times Sarah and I had, Mom," she said, pretending to sniffle. "I really miss her."

Her mother nodded sadly. "So do I, dear, so do I."

Cannibal Cave

I f she screamed loud enough she could hear the echoes bouncing off the walls of caverns far below, something she never tired of doing. Since the day she discovered the cave near her home, Keri spent nearly every waking moment exploring its nooks and crannies. She loved the bats who screeched about, flying every which way. And she'd once found an old arrowhead, proving that Indians had used the cave long ago.

"Honestly, Keri," her mother said. "I don't know why you want to crawl around in some smelly old cave. It's so unladylike."

"So is baseball, Mom."

"That's different, sweetheart. You should be able to play just like the boys."

Gotcha, Keri thought. "Then why can't I explore the cave, too?"

Her mother opened her mouth to speak and realized she had no logical argument. It was her father who ruined it all.

"Because it's dangerous, hon. Anything could happen down there: a rock slide, a cave-in . . . anything. Your mother and I don't want you going there anymore."

But Keri didn't listen and kept returning to the underground world she loved. Then one day, in a secret chamber, she found the remains of half-eaten animals and it made her nervous for the first time. What if some monster lurked there, ready to pounce on her? After that, the cave seemed both more scary and more attractive. Then she read the story.

The old book sat up on the top shelf of her parent's library where she found it one rainy day. It had scary stories, stories about monsters and other creepy things. Normally, she would have read them and forgotten them, but there was one called "Cannibal Cave."

It told about a young boy who, like her, loved to play in a cave near his home. One day a monster caught him and ate him alive, leaving only his bones.

"Gross," she said, slamming the book closed.

"What's wrong, dear?" her mother called from the kitchen.

"Nothing, Ma."

But it wasn't nothing. She lay awake all night imagining herself back in the cave, running, screaming, from a monstrous scaly beast with a million teeth and hot, smelly breath.

The next morning, though, as the sun peeked through her window, it all seemed dumb and childish. Those bones in the cave were probably the remains of some sick cat or dog who'd crawled inside to die. It was stupid to let some story keep her away from her favorite place.

That afternoon, she dropped off her school books, grabbed her flashlight, and headed back to the cave. Once inside, the familiar sights, smells, and sounds calmed her. She began looking for arrowheads. She was so intent on her search, she didn't hear someone creeping up behind her. She screamed when the hand fell on her shoulder. Whirling in fright, she lost her balance and fell, twisting her ankle beneath her. She cried out again as a white-hot pain shot up her leg. Then, in the beam of her fallen flashlight, Keri caught sight of a stooped figure lurching toward her.

"Sorry, Missy," the old tramp said, holding up his arms to calm her. "I didn't mean to scare you. I was just a might curious to see who was sharin' my digs. You okay?"

"You—you mean, you *live* here?" she asked, still reeling from the pain.

"Well, at least for a couple of days. It sure beats the outside air for these creaky old bones, anyway."

He came closer and Keri winced as his gentle hands probed her injury. "Bone's not broke," the old

tramp said, "but you sure twisted that ankle good. You won't be runnin' no marathons anytime soon, but you'll be okay."

More calm now, Keri allowed herself to examine the old man more closely. He appeared to be no older than fifty, but his wild white hair and scraggly beard made him look far older. His clothes, mostly rags, stank of dried sweat and ground-in filth. When he smiled, Keri saw that he had only three teeth. In spite of his ghastly appearance, he didn't seem quite so scary anymore.

"I'm sorry I screamed, but I've been a little jumpy since I read this story the other day."

The old tramp smiled and nodded. "That wouldn't be 'Cannibal Cave,' would it?"

The old man cackled softly as he saw Keri's eyes widen in surprise.

"You *know* that story?" she asked.

"Why sure. Read it when I was no older than you. That and everythin' like it. I was a regular horror fanatic. And as you can see, it more or less rubbed off on me. I sure gave you a fright, didn't I?"

He laughed again and Keri joined in, forgetting the throbbing in her ankle. For the first time since meeting the old tramp, Keri felt that she'd found an ally.

"Name's Gabby," he said, sticking out his hand.

Keri tried to get up, but found her ankle was too weak to support her. "I'm Keri," she said, sinking to the floor of the cave.

"Well, Keri, you'd best sit awhile. How 'bout stayin' for supper?"

Keri felt her stomach twist as she imagined what Gabby must be eating. "Uhh, no, thanks. Maybe I—"

Just then, they heard heavy breathing and saw the light of a torch coming into view. Another old tramp appeared, looking even more frightening than her new-found friend.

"Aha!" he said, grinning madly as his gaze fell on Keri. "Dinner, dinner, dinner!"

Gabby stepped in front of Keri protectively and grabbed her flashlight for a weapon. "You get on outta here!" he hollered at the other tramp. "Or I'll bust your head wide open, I will."

The other tramp growled and stalked off, leaving Keri and Gabby alone.

"When you're on your own, you gots to look out for number one," he said, fixing the injured girl with a wild-eyed stare. "I was gettin' so tired of eatin' them cats and dogs. But you'll make a right tasty stew, yessiree."

Friends Forever

The mirror came with the new house and Judy had taken to it immediately. It was one of those freestanding oval mirrors set into a beautiful wooden frame, and Judy found herself gazing into it for hours. It reflected the frilly lace curtains and dainty canopied bed of her new room. And somehow the world inside the mirror looked better to her than the real world around her.

This was the third time in a year they'd moved, and Judy had gotten to the point where she didn't bother making friends. She knew it was only a matter of time before her father announced that his company was moving them again, and it hurt too much to leave friends behind.

"Judy! Come downstairs, sweetheart. Lunch is ready."

"All right, Mom," she called back.

As she started leaving the room, someone whispered her name.

She whirled around. Someone was in her room!

"*Judy,*" the breathy voice called softly, sweetly, almost as if it were a fragrance rather than a sound.

"Who said that?" Judy asked, her eyes darting around the room.

When no one answered, she shrugged and went

downstairs to lunch. She was probably just tired.

But later, after lunch, as she was trying to read, she couldn't stop thinking about that odd voice. She knew she had heard it, so why did it feel like it was all in her head? Curious, she walked over to the mirror and peered at her reflection. She heard the voice again.

"Judy," it said. *"Come and play."*

Staring harder into the mirror, she saw a dark-haired girl about twelve—her own age.

"Who are you?" Judy gasped.

The girl smiled.

"I'm Lilith. Come inside and play," she said. *"There are no grown-ups to bother us here."*

Haltingly, Judy reached out and touched the glass.

"Ooh!" she said, pulling her hand back. Her skin tingled, like it had gone to sleep.

Lilith called to her again. *"Don't be afraid, Judy. Just step inside. Once you come in here, we can be friends forever."*

Judy didn't have to think about it very long. She wasn't happy in the real world and it *had* to be better inside the mirror world. So, taking a deep breath, Judy stepped toward the mirror. Again her skin tingled as she touched the glass, but the mirror was as solid as ever.

"I can't get through, Lilith," Judy said, her heart sinking.

The dark-haired girl smiled.

"I'll make a crack and you can slip through."

Lilith raised one pale white finger and gently touched the glass. Instantly, a crack appeared and Judy

slipped through into the mirror world.

For what seemed like hours, Judy played with her new friend. She was having the best time, but soon she started getting tired. "I think I'm ready to go home now," she told Lilith. "Where's the mirror so I can get back? Why can't I see it?"

Lilith smiled. *"You can only see the mirror when I want you to see it. But why do you want to go? We're having so much fun."*

"I know, but I have to," Judy said, walking away. "My mom will worry."

"But we're friends forever," insisted Lilith. *"You can't go back."* Then, with reptilian speed, the dark-haired girl reached out and snatched Judy's wrist in a grip that felt like cold steel.

Horrified, Judy whirled around and tried to get away, but Lilith held her with ease.

"Let me go!" Judy yelled, pulling with all her strength.

Lilith just stared at her, a sad smile on her face. *"All I want is to be friends with you . . . friends forever."*

Suddenly Judy heard her mother's voice coming from somewhere far away. "Oh, no," her mother was saying. "There's a crack running through Judy's mirror. She'll be heartbroken. Well, she's probably out making new friends. I'll just get it replaced before she gets back."

"NOOOOO!" Judy screamed. She turned to Lilith and smashed her square in the face with her fist.

A crystalline tear ran down Lilith's cheek, and then a blissful smile rose to her lips. *"I'm very happy* to have you as my friend, Judy. And you might as well get used to being my friend. Once your mother replaces the magic mirror with a regular one, you'll be with me here forever."

"MOTHERRRRR!" Judy wailed. "DON'T CHANGE THE MIRROR!"

But her mother heard nothing. She was already on the phone giving the measurements for a new mirror to the man at the glass shop.

"Now, I need this delivered as soon as possible," she was saying. "My daughter's out with new friends and I want the old mirror replaced by the time she gets back."

Deadly Dreams

as Great-Grandfather Norris really a cowboy?" Chester asked. He was awed by his legendary namesake.

His father smiled at him while he cleaned and oiled the old pair of six-guns that hung over the fireplace.

"Uh-huh. He rode alongside General Custer and was the only survivor of the Battle of Little Big Horn."

"Wow!" exclaimed Chester, his eyes wide. "What else did he do?"

"Well, let's see," his father said, squinting his eyes in thought. "He was Deputy Marshall of Deadwood, Colorado later that same year. Wild Bill Hickock was his boss and his best buddy, and your great-grandpa saw old Bill get killed right before his eyes. See these notches?" he asked, showing Chester one of the six-guns.

Chester leaned forward and looked at the handles of the pistols. Sure enough, he saw half a dozen grooves carved into the old wood.

"Those stand for all the bad guys your great-grandpa killed in the course of his duty."

"When did he die?"

"That's the strange part," his father said, shoving the pistols back into the old leather gun belt. "He disappeared one day and no one ever saw him again. His wife looked high and low, but gave up after a year. She figured someone had bushwhacked him on the trail and buried the body."

Chester tried to concentrate in school all the next day, but found himself daydreaming about dusty streets at high noon, blazing gun battles, and weeping widows. On the bus ride home that afternoon, sun blasted through the window, making him drowsy. He soon drifted off into a deep sleep.

Jolted awake by a bump in the road, Chester opened his eyes and gasped. He was no longer on the bus, but seated inside a creaky stagecoach bouncing along a dusty road. Across from him sat a tall, sweaty man, his cheek stuffed with chewing tobacco. The man had on a long, grimy coat, a wrinkled shirt with a soiled collar and stained tie, and baggy red-and-white plaid pants. Perched on his head was a battered top hat, the crown frayed and worn. The man spit a stream of brown tobacco juice out the window and grinned. His teeth were the color of chocolate.

"Hey, boy. You headed for Deadwood?" the man asked.

Before Chester could answer, the stage rattled to a stop and the driver yelled down through the hole in the roof.

"Here we are, laddie, right where you wanted to go."

Chester's stomach churned as he stepped onto the road. The sun hit him with a blast of blazing heat, searing his skin and making him squint. Slowly his eyes adjusted and he scanned the town.

It looked like a million other small western towns

he'd seen in the movies: a wide, dusty street with sun-bleached two-story buildings on either side, a saloon, sheriff's office and jail, general store, and a post office. At the far end of town, he saw a crowd gathered under a stout old oak tree.

"What's going on?" he asked one of the men on the outskirts of the crowd.

"A hangin'. Can't you see that?" the man said, annoyed.

"Who're you hanging?"

The man ignored the question, more interested in Chester's brightly colored sneakers and baggy-legged shorts.

"Those are mighty peculiar duds you got on. You from back East?"

"Sort of . . . I guess. Who're you hanging?" he asked again.

The man chuckled. "Well, son, he's the meanest man in the West, but that ain't what we're hangin' him for. That is, if we hang him. The judge is on his way here right now and I hear tell he might just let that son-of-a-gun go. In a way, I sort o' hope old Chester makes it."

"What did you say?" the boy asked in disbelief.

"I said, I hope old Chester makes it."

"Chester who?"

The man looked annoyed again. "Why, Norris, of course!"

"Grandpa!" Chester whispered.

Chester dove into the crowd and muscled his way through to the center. There he saw a man on horse-back, his hands tied behind him, and a noose around

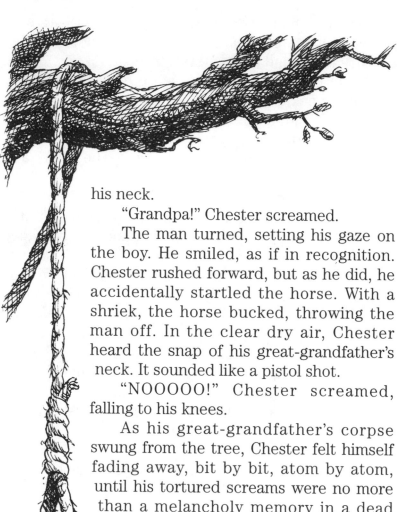

his neck.

"Grandpa!" Chester screamed.

The man turned, setting his gaze on the boy. He smiled, as if in recognition. Chester rushed forward, but as he did, he accidentally startled the horse. With a shriek, the horse bucked, throwing the man off. In the clear dry air, Chester heard the snap of his great-grandfather's neck. It sounded like a pistol shot.

"NOOOOO!" Chester screamed, falling to his knees.

As his great-grandfather's corpse swung from the tree, Chester felt himself fading away, bit by bit, atom by atom, until his tortured screams were no more than a melancholy memory in a dead man's dreams.

The Glass Eye

I t stared back at him from a jar of mixed marbles. Nearly twice as big as an aggie, it looked nothing like the other brightly colored spheres of glass. It was an eye. And a blue eye, at that. Crisscrossed by tiny red veins, it immediately grabbed Tony's attention.

Ever since he could walk, Tony loved to spend time inside Thompson's Emporium. It was filled with all kinds of things from floor to ceiling, and Tony would spend hours digging out the occasional gem from all the junk. Even when not there, he could close his eyes and wander down those aisles, his nose filled with that wonderful musty scent.

"How much for the eye?" he said, moving along the high wooden counter.

Mr. Thompson leaned over and peered into the jar, squinting through his thick glasses. He reached inside the jar, pulled out the eye, and plopped it onto the dusty counter. "Well, so you're the lucky one to find this treasure," he said. "And because you must be special, I'll sell it to ya for the grand price of a dollar."

The eye gleamed invitingly in the mellow light and Tony found himself sorely tempted. All he *had* was a dollar and that was for a new comic book he'd been craving. But this eye was very cool. All his friends

would drool over it for sure. He pulled out his wrinkled
dollar and handed it to the old storekeeper. Plucking
the eye off the counter, Tony walked out of the store,
eager to show off his prize.

82

"That's a really neat eye," Freddy Richards said, rolling it in his hands. "But it's got a nick in it."

"What!" Tony said, snatching it back. Sure enough, he could see a small imperfection on the back. Tony held it up to his eye and was startled to see that he could look through it. Everything looked different, like it glowed or something. As he scanned the street, he saw a woman come out of the grocery store and bump into a man walking down the sidewalk. The woman gave out a startled screech and fell to the ground, her packages scattering.

Tony laughed. "Did you see that woman?"

"What woman?" Freddy asked, looking confused.

"That woman, across the street—"

Tony looked again and saw no one in front of the store.

"Maybe you should get your *own* eyes checked," Freddy said, laughing as he ran off.

Tony shook his head, about to walk away, when the woman—the same woman he saw moments before—came walking out of the grocery store again! Tony watched, his breath coming in excited gasps, as the woman collided with the man exactly as before. Only this time he knew it was real.

Trembling, he ran home, his hand tightly gripping the eye so as not to break it.

"Look through it, if you don't believe me," he said to his parents.

"Honey, it's just a glass eye, nothing more."

Tony held up the eye and looked through the glass. Everything looked the same. Maybe his parents were right. He was just about to stop looking through

83

the eye when he saw his mother kneeling on the floor, wiping up the remains of a spill.

"I'd be careful with dinner, Mom," Tony said, smiling broadly. "Your pot roast is headed for the floor."

His mother laughed. "What on earth are you talking about?" she asked. "Oh, well, I guess that imagination of yours can't be stopped."

She got up and went into the kitchen. Tony waited. He wanted to warn his mother again, but—

"OOOUUUCH!"

The clatter of the pot hitting the floor made Tony smile even wider. "See?" said Tony.

Tony's father shook his head. "Son, that doesn't prove anything. Your mother just had an accident. That's all."

"But I *saw* it," Tony insisted.

"Just your imagination. I used to see things like that all the time when I was your age."

Feeling stupid, Tony trudged over to the dinner table, dropped into his chair, and moped. His father's expression softened.

"Say, sport, how about we go and get some ice cream after dinner?"

"Okay, Dad," Tony said, nodding absently.

Maybe it was just a stupid piece of glass. He'd take it back to Old Man Thompson and get his money tomorrow. He turned to his father, smiled, and said, "Rocky Road with fudge sauce?"

"You're on, kiddo," his father replied.

As Tony's mother cleared the table sometime later, she noticed the eye sitting there, staring at her. She felt a shiver course through her. Wasn't it strange that

Tony had known she would drop the roast? Could it be? Could the eye have some kind of power?

"Ridiculous," she said, starting to walk away. She halted after a couple of steps and turned back. With curiosity overcoming her reluctance, she picked up the eye and brought it up to her own.

She gasped as she saw herself walking out the front door. What on earth? More than curious, she ran to the door, opened it, and walked out into the twilight. She stood on the sidewalk and once again brought the glass eye up to her own. She laughed as she spotted her husband's car turning onto their street.

"Peekaboo, I see you," she giggled.

And then it happened. She saw herself running into the street, waving her arms as a pickup truck, driven by someone obviously drunk, swerved out of a side street, on a sure collision course with her husband's car.

Screaming, she dropped the glass eye and ran into the street, just as her husband's car turned the corner. She screamed and screamed, yet the car continued onward toward disaster. Panicking, she ran farther into the street, farther than she'd seen herself go while looking through the glass eye. She never saw the other car as it ran her down; she never saw her husband swerve just in time to miss a sure and fiery death.

Scarecrow

is father held him high up on his shoulders as Kirk pinned the two buttons on the straw figure.

"Now, be sure to put those buttons on just right, son. A scarecrow's got to have real fierce eyes or the crows will just laugh at it. And we can't have our scarecrow bein' laughed at, can we?"

Kirk shook his head. "No, sir," he said, placing the two black-pearl buttons just so.

The scarecrow, now complete, hung on its wooden post in the middle of a vast cornfield, its arms open to the limitless sky. Kirk smiled with pleasure at his handiwork. He liked being up here with the scarecrow. He could look across the tops of the cornstalks and see almost the whole world.

"Let's go see what your ma is cooking for dinner," Kirk's father said, bounding through the rows of corn. Kirk laughed as he bounced along on the man's wide shoulders. Turning, he looked back at the scarecrow's fierce expression and saw a lone crow flapping away, cawing in fright.

"You're quite a scarecrow maker, boy," his father remarked a few days later.

Kirk smiled proudly. "I like scarecrows, Daddy. They're neat."

His father nodded thoughtfully. "Well, there might

be some other folks in the county who might need your special touch. I'll ask around."

Sure enough, Old Man Parsons, who owned the farm up the road, needed a scarecrow. So again, he sat on his father's shoulders and put the eyes on just like he'd done when he finished the scarecrow in his father's fields. The black-pearl buttons gleamed in the blazing sun, seemingly alive with dark intent. Immediately a family of crows began cawing in protest, taking flight and soaring away. Old Man Parsons beamed with delight.

"You were right, Ezra, the boy's got the touch."

"Yep," Ezra said, nodding proudly, patting Kirk on the back.

As the days passed, news of Kirk's special touch spread around the county. Farmer after farmer asked him to come and make scarecrows for them. On some, he needed only to put on the eyes; others he made from scratch, picking out the clothes and stuffing in the straw all by himself. Everyone marveled at the young boy's talent. And never had the corn looked so green as it did now.

"Kirk?" his mother said one day. "Have you seen my box of black-pearl buttons?"

Kirk swallowed, his eyes wide with guilt.

"I'm sorry, Momma. I used 'em for my scarecrows' eyes."

His mother sighed and sank onto the sofa. "Those buttons belonged to your great-grandmother. They came all the way from Africa and have been handed down in my family for generations. I was going to pass them on to your older sister."

Kirk felt heartbroken as he saw the tears in his mother's eyes. "Here," he said pulling his hand out of his pocket. There on his open palm lay the last two buttons.

His mother smiled. "It's okay, sweetheart. You keep them. Maybe they'll bring you better luck than they did Great-Grandma. She died mysteriously while sewing the buttons on a new dress."

Kirk felt just horrible when he went to bed that night. He would never have used those buttons if he'd known. But they'd made such great eyes for the scarecrows. And if the truth be told, he figured they had a lot to do with how well all the scarecrows worked. There was something spooky about the way those buttons shone out of the cloth faces.

* * *

The cawing of a crow woke him up, but that wasn't what made Kirk's heart pound and his throat go dry. His room was filled with crows. Hundreds of them. They stood on the sill of the open window, they perched on the brass rails of his bed, they squatted on his footlocker and roosted on his dresser. Everywhere he looked, Kirk saw crows. They watched him, silent as a tomb, their beady amber eyes boring into him. He could feel their hatred; he could sense their ravenous hunger for the corn denied them by his miraculous scarecrows.

Scared witless, Kirk tried to crawl out of bed, recoiling as his bare feet touched a mass of feathered bodies teeming on the floor. Suddenly the air became charged with a heavy, almost electric atmosphere. All at once, the crows began flapping their wings. It sounded like thunder.

And then they fell upon him.

* * *

The rooster crowed at dawn, waking Ezra from a sound slumber. Pulling on his clothes, he bent down to kiss his wife and saw, out of the corner of his eye, something strange in the field. Grabbing his shotgun, he ran out to the scarecrow.

"NOOOO!" he screamed, falling to his knees.

There, hanging from the scarecrow's perch, was Kirk's horribly broken body, straw sticking out from everywhere. But the sight Ezra would take to his grave were those black-pearl buttons stuck in the bloody holes where his son's eyes used to be.

The Wishing Star

Why can't I have a kitten?" Raymond asked.

His mother sighed and put down her briefcase, weary from a hard day.

"We've been over this a hundred times, honey," she said. "Our landlord doesn't allow pets and your father is allergic to them."

"We can get the hairless kind. I read all about them. Dad'll be fine."

"How fine will we be out on the street if Mr. Maxon finds out? I'm sorry, Raymond, but a tiny apartment in Brooklyn is a terrible place for a pet."

Raymond nodded sadly, realizing his mother was right. But he still yearned to have a cute little ball of fur he could call his own. That night, as he lay in bed, he stared out the window and noticed an odd pulsing star high up in the heavens. That was strange. He'd never noticed it before. Maybe he should wish on it for a kitten. But no, he'd get in big trouble.

"Sorry, Wishing Star. Nothing for me tonight."

The next day, a dirty stray kitten followed him home. No matter how hard he tried to make it go away, it stuck right by him. It was as if the Wishing Star had looked deep inside him and read his true desires. Scared of discovery, but happy, Raymond tucked the kitten under his coat and snuck it into the basement of his building. There he gave it a bath, named it Homer, and arranged a litter box for it behind the boiler.

"Now, Homer, you be good, or Mr. Maxon will throw us out."

The next morning he found five more cats had joined Homer.

"Oh no!" Raymond said, his pulse racing. "What am I going to do now?"

He sprinted out of the building with the cats trailing behind him. Everywhere he went, the cats followed, joined by others of every kind. There were so many following him that by the day's end, Raymond had lost count. And every day it got worse. When he crossed the street, they tied up traffic. Neighbors complained about the fights and the howling at night. Finally, at the landlord's frantic request, Officer Summers came knocking.

"What are you feeding those cats?" the burly cop demanded.

Raymond felt a stab of fear as he saw his mother frown. "I'm not feeding them anything. They just like me."

"Well, you'll have to get rid of them, or I might have to run you down to the station."

The policeman winked at his mother, something Raymond missed in his blind panic.

That night, he saw the strange star again. Somehow it looked bigger, brighter.

"Maybe you misunderstood me, Wishing Star. I don't want any cats. I wish you'd take them away."

The next morning, Raymond was relieved to find the cats gone. But his relief turned to alarm as a small, sad-eyed puppy followed him home from school.

"Where did you come from?" he asked the adorable puppy. And then he remembered—when he'd asked for the Wishing Star to take the cats away, the thought of having a puppy had run through his mind. Now dogs began flocking to Raymond, just as the cats had. As if he were some kind of giant dog biscuit, they dutifully followed him everywhere, barking, running, and howling at his heels. As before, Raymond's tight-knit neighborhood flew into an uproar and once again Officer Summers came calling. This time, he was not so nice.

"Now, I warned you once, kid, and I'm not about to warn you again. You're creating a nuisance. I'll see you in Juvenile Hall if you don't stop all this nonsense!"

The cop turned and left, all red-faced and blustery.

"Raymond? What do you have to say for yourself?" his mother asked.

Raymond looked at her, feeling helpless. "I'm sorry, Mom. I can't help it if these animals like me."

His mother gazed at him, her expression cool and distant. "Raymond, I think you should go to your room and think about what you've done."

"But I didn't *do* anything!" he whined.

Feeling sad and angry, he ran back to his room and shut the door. Why were grown-ups so stupid sometimes?

He trudged to the window and sank to his knees, staring up into the twinkling sky. It took only a moment for him to spot that familiar pulsing star. Seeing it brought back all the bad memories of the last few days. "Wishing Star—why does everything I want get all messed up?"

The star twinkled, remaining silent.

Raymond shook his head. That was stupid. Did he expect the star to talk, too?

"Wishing Star? I wish you'd take away the dogs," he said, pausing to listen. He smiled as the constant barking slowly faded away. But the star kept on twinkling, almost as if it were trying to make him make another wish. Raymond got angry. "You're not going to get me into any more trouble. In fact, I wish you'd go away, too!"

Suddenly the star exploded, its energy rapidly

expanding outward like ripples on a lake. Its light grew so bright, it hurt his eyes to look at it. Raymond clamped them shut, opening them a moment later. As his vision cleared, he looked upward and saw only blackness where the Wishing Star had been. Feeling happy and relieved, he climbed into bed and fell into a deep, dreamless sleep.

That night, as Raymond slept, he never felt the energy from the exploded star as it rammed into the earth and shattered the planet into a billion fiery fragments . . .

Index